W9-BKS-935

DATE			

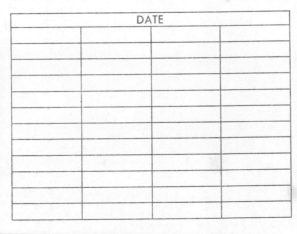

Hannah the Hippo's
No Mud Day

Hannah the Hippo's No Mud Day

By Iris Hiskey
Illustrated by Karen Lee Schmidt

SIMON AND SCHUSTER BOOKS FOR YOUNG READERS
Published by Simon & Schuster Inc.
New York · London · Toronto · Sydney · Tokyo · Singapore

SIMON AND SCHUSTER BOOKS FOR YOUNG READERS
Simon & Schuster Building, Rockefeller Center,
1230 Avenue of the Americas, New York, New York 10020

The text of this book is set in 17 pt. Fournier.
The display type is Post Roman Light.
The illustrations were done in watercolor
on 300 lb. Arches Hot Press paper.

Designed by Vicki Kalajian

Manufactured in Hong Kong

10 9 8 7 6 5 4 3 2 1

Library of Congress Cataloging-in-Publication Data
Hiskey, Iris.   Hannah the Hippo's no mud day /
by Iris Hiskey; illustrated by Karen Lee Schmidt.
p.   cm.   Summary: Hannah the Hippo finds she
cannot stay clean even on the day her Aunt Lily
is coming to visit.
[1. Hippopotamus—Fiction.   2. Aunts—Fiction.]
I. Schmidt, Karen Lee, ill.   II. Title.
PZ7.A7343Han   1991   [E]—dc20
90-37071
ISBN 0-671-69194-5

For my mudpuddlers, Max and Zachary
—I.H.

For Cody Dieruf, a fine poet and artist
—K.L.S.

"Guess what, Hannah Banana," said Mama Hippo one morning as she cleared away the breakfast dishes. "Something wonderful is going to happen today."

"What?" asked Hannah.

"My little sister Lily is coming for a visit," said Mama Hippo.

"The one who's been traveling all over the world for years and years?" asked Hannah.

"Yes," said Mama Hippo. "She hasn't seen you since you were a baby. So now it's time to jump into a nice bubbly bath. I want you to look clean and pretty for your Aunt Lily."

Mama Hippo rubbed and scrubbed Hannah until she was squeaky, shiny clean. Then she brought out a stiff new pink dress with a lacy white pinafore.

"Listen carefully, Hannah," she said. "Today is a *No Mud Day*."

Now this was very bad news for Hannah, because squshy, mushy mud puddles were her favorite things in the world. She loved to dance and prance in the muddy water and to roll about in the gooey mud until she was covered from her nose to her toes. So when Hannah was all clean and dressed in her stiff pink dress with the lacy white pinafore, she was a cross little hippo indeed.

"Now remember, Hannah Banana," said Mama Hippo. "No mud today. Not one tiny speck."

Hannah sighed loudly and sat down on the front porch. It was a hot day. The pink dress itched her neck. She scowled.

Soon her mother peeked out the door. "Why don't you walk down the road as far as the big rocks and see if you can see Aunt Lily coming?" she asked.

Hannah sighed again, but she climbed off the porch and started down the road. *Trudge, trudge, trudge.*

"No mud, no mud, no mud," her feet seemed to say.

Around the first bend in the road, a large mud puddle was waiting. Hannah frowned. She took two steps towards the puddle. Then she took three steps back.

"I can't, I can't, I can't!" she said firmly to herself. She walked carefully around the mud puddle without getting one drop on the stiff pink dress or the lacy white pinafore.

She walked on—*trudge, trudge, trudge*—up a hill, down a hill, around another bend. After a while she came to the big rocks. There was no sign of Aunt Lily. Hannah sat down to wait. Soon she felt so hot and itchy that she decided to go home and sit under a tree in the shade. Then she thought of the mud puddle in the road.

"Oh dear!" she exclaimed. "I can't walk past that one
more time without going in. I'll have to go through
the fields."

Hannah walked off the road. She saw two butterflies
chasing each other. Hannah danced behind, swooping
and gliding with them.

Suddenly she heard a *squish, squash, sqush*. She looked down. Her feet had danced her right into the biggest, muddiest puddle she had ever seen!

Hannah jumped back out of the mud quickly. But how could she waste this extra special mud puddle? Before she knew what she was doing, she had slipped out of the stiff pink dress with the lacy white pinafore, folded it neatly and placed it on the dry grass.

"I'll only go in for a minute," she thought, "and just up to my knees." But the mud was so cool that Hannah just had to dance a little...and then she just had to prance a little...and then she just had to lie down for a second...and then she had to roll over just once...and then...

When she finally climbed out of the puddle, Hannah was covered with mud.

"I'll roll in the grass," she said to herself, "until I roll all the mud off."

She rolled and rolled. Then she rolled some more. But she was still a muddy little hippo.

"Oh no!" she cried. "Mama will be so angry!"

Then she had an idea. She would go to the big river and *wash* the mud off.

Hannah carefully picked up the pink dress with the lacy white pinafore in her teeth and set off. When she got to the river, she saw that there had been a mudslide and the bank was so steep that she couldn't get down to the water.

Hannah stood on the bank and watched two big elephants playing in the river. They splashed about squirting water out of their long trunks. Then Hannah heard a grunting sound nearby. A smaller elephant was trying to climb up the bank.

"I told my brothers I was big enough to get lunch for them," he huffed up at Hannah, "but the bank is too steep for me."

Tears welled up in the little elephant's eyes and he sniffed loudly. Hannah carefully put her pink dress with the lacy white pinafore down on the grass.

"Please don't cry," she said. "I'll help you."

"You will?" said the little elephant, wiping a tear off with his trunk.

"If I can," said Hannah. "What do you need?"

"I need some branches and leaves," said the little elephant, "or some fruit, if you can find it."

Hannah searched about. She found some branches and some juicy-looking leaves. Then she found some bananas and some mangoes. She carried them all back to the river bank and threw them down to the elephant.

"A feast!" he cried. "Oh, thank you!" He trumpeted happily and his brothers came splashing over.

"I wish I could help *you* now," he said to Hannah.

Hannah had been thinking.

"You can," she said. "If you squirt me with clean water from the river, this mud will wash off and I can go home and see my Aunt Lily who's coming for a special visit today."

The elephants filled their trunks with water and squirted and squirted until Hannah was as clean as when she had jumped out of her bathtub that morning.

"Now I can get dressed and go home," she said. She reached down for her pink dress with the lacy white pinafore.

"Oh no!" she cried.

The dress was soaking wet from all the squirting! Hannah tried to wring the water out. She twisted and twisted, but the dress was still wet and now it was crumpled as well.

"This is too much!" cried Hannah. She thought in a moment she would just have to cry. Then she heard some chirping voices.

"Pull harder!"
"I can't get any!"
"Let me try!"

Hannah looked around. Two brightly
colored birds were pulling at the long grass.

"Oh dear, I can't either!"
"We'll never do it!"

"What's wrong?" Hannah asked.

"It will soon be time for me to lay my eggs,"
said one of the birds, "and our nest isn't
strong enough for our babies."

"We need this tough grass, but we can't pull it up," said the other.

"Why that's no problem for me," said Hannah. "I'll pull up as much as you want."

She tore up great hunks of grass.

"That's plenty!" cried one of the birds. "Thank you!"

"Why do you look so sad on such a beautiful hot day?" asked the other bird.

"My new pink dress is all wet and crumpled and Mama will be angry with me," Hannah said.

"Don't worry," said the birds. "We will take your dress and fly with it through the air. The sun will dry it and the warm air will smooth out all the wrinkles."

The birds plucked up the pink dress with the lacy white pinafore in their beaks and soared high into the sunny sky. Back and forth they flew with the dress streaming out behind them. In no time at all they landed at Hannah's feet and the dress was dry and smooth.

"Oh thank you!" she cried, slipping it on. "It looks perfect and it's not even stiff any more!" So, clean and dry once again, Hannah set off for home.

"Why Hannah, you really, really did it,"
said Mama Hippo hugging her tight.
"There's not one drop of mud on you!"
Hannah blushed.
"Well," she said, "actually..."
Suddenly there was a loud shout.
"HALLOOOO!"
Hannah looked down the road and
her eyes nearly popped out.

Aunt Lily bustled up to Hannah and Mama Hippo and gave them huge hugs and kisses.

"Whew!" she said, pulling off her shawl. "There's just one thing to do on a hot day like this."

"What's that?" asked Hannah shyly.

"Take a nice cool roll in the mud!" cried Aunt Lily, wriggling out of her clothes. "Know any good spots?"

"Well," said Hannah, smiling from ear to ear, "as a matter of fact, I do!"